Say hello to the Bunnykins!

Written by Nicola Baxter
Illustrated by Frank Endersby

Manufactured under licence by
Bookmart Limited, Desford Road, Enderby, Leicester LE9 5AD

Published by Bookmart Limited
Registered Number 2372865
Trading as Bookmart Limited
Desford Road Enderby Leicester LE9 5AD

ISBN 1-85605-920-0

Produced for Bookmart Limited by Nicola Baxter
PO Box 71 Diss Norfolk IP22 2DT

Designed by Amanda Hawkes

Printed in Singapore

By
Royal Doulton

Tom's Twin Trouble

AND

Harry's Huge Hat

Tom's Twin Trouble

Sometimes Tom wasn't at all sure he liked being a twin. Of course, he loved his brother Harry, and it was often fun to play tricks on grown-ups who couldn't tell one twin from the other. But as the twins grew older, there were problems, too.

For example, not long ago, Father had made a beautiful swing for the little bunnies and hung it on a big, old apple tree in the garden. Tom loved to swing on it. If he swung really high, he could see right over the fence and out towards the fields and the stream beyond. He could imagine he was a famous pilot, swooping over the countryside far below.

But when Tom had been swinging for about five minutes, the same thing always happened. “It’s my turn now!” Harry would call.

And nine times out of ten, Mother or Father Bunnykins would hear the noise and say, “Give your brother a turn, Tom. It’s only fair.”

Exactly the same thing happened if Tom sat down with one of his favourite books. Although the little bunnies had lots of lovely books to read, Harry always decided he wanted to look at that very same book *right now.*

And that is why, I'm sorry to say, sometimes Tom and Harry seemed to do more squabbling than all the other little bunnies put together.

"I don't know what's the matter with those two," said Mother Bunnykins one evening, when the little ones were in bed and there was peace at last.

"I do," said Father Bunnykins. "My brother was not very much younger than me, and we were always annoying each other. It didn't matter what I wanted to do, he always wanted to do it as well. We couldn't find anything to do together that didn't end in some sort of quarrel."

"What happened?" asked Mother Bunnykins. "You get on so well, now."

"Ah," sighed Father Bunnykins, "that's because my dear old Dad came up with a brilliant idea. He made us something we could both play with, and we were soon the best of friends. And if you'll excuse me, my dear, I'm going out into my workshop to make one for *our* two terrors." And he went out to his workshop in the garage, where he worked on Secret Projects.

Father Bunnykins worked late into the night. As she drifted off to sleep, Mother Bunnykins could hear sawing, and hammering, and an odd creaking noise. And some of it seemed to be coming from the garden, which was even more puzzling.

Next morning, as Father Bunnykins rubbed his sleepy eyes in front of the bedroom window, he saw that the terrible twins had already discovered their surprise, and were having a wonderful time!

"The great thing about a seesaw," he told Mother Bunnykins, "is that you need *two* little bunnies to make it work."

"And they're six feet apart," laughed Mother Bunnykins, "which is even better!"

Harry's Huge Hat

Harry and Tom loved going to nursery school. Lots of their friends went, too, and there were always lots of exciting things to do. Tom loved all the running and jumping and climbing games. Harry preferred the quiet afternoons when all the little bunnies made pictures, or models, or pretty little pots to take home to their mothers.

On the last spring afternoon before the holidays, Mrs Whiskers, the teacher, announced that today the girls would be making Easter bonnets and the boys would be making models of the Easter Bunny.

Everyone set to work at once. But in the hustle and bustle, Harry sat still.

"What is it, Harry?" asked Mrs Whiskers. "Don't you want to make a model of the Easter Bunny? You're so good at making things."

As Harry didn't say anything, Mrs Whiskers tried to encourage him some more. "I'm sure your Bunny would be lovely. You could take it home and put it on the table on Easter Day."

But Harry still didn't hurry to get his clay and modelling tools. Instead, he looked up at his teacher and said, very softly, "May I whisper, Mrs Whiskers?"

"Yes, of course, Harry," said the teacher, crouching down beside him. "What did you want to tell me?"

"Well," whispered Harry, "I'd much rather make an Easter bonnet than an Easter Bunny."

Mrs Whiskers was surprised. "Er … do you think you'd look nice in an Easter bonnet, Harry?" she asked.

Harry's little nose went pink. "Of course not!" he said, out loud this time. "I want to make it for Mother. She was only saying the other day that her best hat had holes in it."

Mrs Whiskers smiled. "I think that's a lovely idea," she said. "Go and find some coloured card and paper. You'll need to make your hat a little larger than the others, you know."

Harry hurried off to find everything he needed. Soon he had coloured card, tissue paper, scissors, glue, ribbons and even some feathers that Mrs Whiskers found at the bottom of her Bits-and-Pieces Box.

“What are you doing?” asked Tom, getting ready to make a joke. But when Harry explained, Tom rather wished he’d had the same idea.

The little bunnies worked all afternoon. At last Mrs Whiskers told them it was time to wash their paws and put all their things away. When everything was clean and tidy, including the little bunnies, they got ready to show Mrs Whiskers all the lovely things they had made.

"Those are very good models and beautiful hats," she said. "Carry them home carefully – and Happy Easter to all of you!"

Harry and Tom walked slowly home. Harry carried his hat very carefully, so that it didn't brush against the hedges or blow away in the breeze.

"Look what we've made for you!" Tom called to Mother Bunnykins, as the two little bunnies wiped their feet on the doormat. They hid their presents behind their backs, which was not too easy in the case of Harry's huge hat.

"What a beautiful Easter Bunny!" cried Mother Bunnykins, looking at what Tom had made. "Let's put it on the windowsill, where everyone can see it. Did you make one too, Harry?"

"No," said Harry shyly. "I made you this!" And, very carefully, he gave her the large and wonderful hat.

"Oh, Harry!" cried Mother Bunnykins. "That is the most beautiful hat I've ever seen! I'm going to try it on at once."

She hurried to the hall mirror and put on the hat. But, oh dear! It was *much* too big!

Poor Harry was near to tears. "It's no good!" he wailed. "You can't wear it like that! I'm so sorry!"

But Mother Bunnykins was smiling. "No, I can't wear it," she said, "but that's a good thing. It would have been awful if it had got wet in the rain or torn on a tree branch. No, the best thing about this hat is…

that I can turn it the other way up and make a beautiful basket for all our Easter eggs! We'll put it right in the middle of the table. Doesn't it look wonderful?"

And, do you know, it did!